There's MAGIC in the BEAR

D1741379

Rosa Frost

There's Magic in the Bear
Copyright © 2015 Rosa Frost

ISBN: 978-1-942508-10-6

Published by Touch Publishing
P.O. Box 180303
Arlington, TX 76096
www.TouchPublishingServices.com

Cover design by Touch Publishing

Library of Congress Control Number: 2015940341

Printed in the United States of America on acid-free paper

For Gregory. Without his love for Ken Bear, this story would never have been written.

For all my family who inspire me daily with their love of life and support of my efforts to chronicle it.

All my love.

Contents

Ken Bear had been with Gregory forever. That is, forever minus the few short weeks he spent in a local shop before Gregory's gramma, who was visiting with his granddad from Texas, found him. She bought him as a companion for Gregory, her first grandson, who was just 3 months old at the time. So you see, it is fair to say that Gregory and Ken Bear had been together for all of their young lives.

If you had been fortunate enough to meet Ken Bear, it would have been apparent at first glance that he was well and truly loved. As a matter of fact, his face was all but loved off! There were great gaping holes where his nice, soft, velvety fur had once been. His nose was held on by mere threads, and was in danger of falling right off his severely tattered face. His smile, which had unraveled over the course of time, was rather lopsided. Gregory's mother had tried to mend it, but Ken

Bear looked as if he were trying to shrug off a pesky fly. If you looked closely, you could see the white, fluffy material inside his head. It was kept in place by a scarce row of vertical threads, doing their very best to hold together.

A futile attempt had been made somewhere along the way to mend the opening in his chest, but the material used didn't match and made him look a bit like a scarecrow. Of course it didn't help that the stuffing peeked out through the stitches at regular intervals and frequently had to be poked back inside.

As time took its toll on Ken Bear's exterior, his self-esteem wore down, too. Each time he caught a glimpse of his reflection in a mirror, he reminded himself that it was just a matter of time until he would end up like most stuffed bears when they fell into disrepair. He would be dropped into a dark, dingy, smelly rubbish bin on his way to a fate that he just couldn't bear to imagine.

As his face and body deteriorated, he found it more and more difficult to remain the cheerful companion he had always been. He knew Gregory still needed him (some days more than others) and if it wasn't for that knowledge, well, he may have just given up altogether.

Then, one day not too very long ago, things started to change for the better. Some will say it was fate, others call it chance, but you and I will know differently.

One Tuesday morning, Gregory forgot to reach for Ken Bear like he usually did when he woke up. Instead, he jumped out of bed, quickly got dressed, and was away down the stairs before Ken Bear even knew it was morning. Poor Ken Bear had to spend the entire day lying in a cramped and uncomfortable position under a crumpled mess of bed linens. It was "Games Day" at school, and Gregory had been too excited to make up his bed. The only thing that kept Ken Bear from losing his cool completely was a large fold in the bedding, which let in some fresh air from the open window. Every so often Ken Bear would feel a gentle puff of wind through the sheets. Unbeknownst to Ken Bear, one of these puffs brought with it something that would forever change life as he knew it.

You see, a bit of magic dust floated in on the wind, circulated down through the opening in the linens, sifted through the threadbare fur on Ken Bear's left cheek, and embedded itself inside him.

As the magic began to take root, a spiral of tiny, magic-dust particles started to swirl and wind around and through the fibers of Ken Bear's being. He was unaware of it, but Ken Bear was about to embark on a wonderful adventure.

As Ken Bear lay there counting the seemingly endless hours in the dark and musty bedcovers, he convinced himself that this was the way it would be from now on. After all, he mused, Gregory was growing up and his life was filling up with other interests. Ken Bear even imagined that Gregory would find another stuffed bear or toy to replace him! One that was new and not so full of holes. One whose nose was firmly attached to a face still soft with fur. He saw himself becoming forgotten and figured he would eventually just cease to exist. Alas, one is hard-pressed to know how all of these thoughts managed to stay inside a head as well-ventilated as his.

All of these thoughts made it a long, long day indeed. By the time Gregory got home that afternoon, Ken Bear had sunk into a deep, dark despair. If Ken Bear could shed tears, the bedclothes would have been a sopping, wet mess!

But, as we all know, stuffed bears cannot shed tears. When their hearts are sad, there is no way for them to let it out, so the pain builds up and eats away at their insides (and, as I've already explained, Ken Bear was already in jeopardy of losing his insides). It was a very sad and miserable Ken Bear who greeted Gregory when he came home from school that day.

When Gregory retrieved Ken Bear out from under the bedclothes, he could feel the sadness in Ken Bear's heart. Gregory studied Ken Bear's face and, although he couldn't be sure, he thought Ken Bear looked rather sad and lonely. Gregory felt badly for rushing off and leaving Ken Bear scrunched up under the covers all day and promised he would never, ever do it again! Ken Bear wanted to believe him, but Ken Bear knew from experience that little boys were good at making promises, but poor at remembering them when something exciting pulled at their coattails.

But at that moment in time, Gregory truly was sorry and wanted to make Ken Bear feel better. He grabbed him up, hugged him tightly against his small chest, and ran as fast as his legs could carry him in search of his mother. Gregory thought perhaps there was something she could do to make Ken Bear feel better again.

Ken Bear was shoved into Gregory's mother's

hands, as he asked her to do *something* to help Ken Bear. Ken Bear listened sadly as Mother said, alas, she had done all she knew to improve Ken Bear's condition. She suggested to Gregory that perhaps it was time for him to put Ken Bear away and find a new companion. After all, she continued, Gregory was going to be ten years old soon and most boys his age had already left their baby toys far behind. She even offered to help him find more grown up activities to spend time on, like sports and playing with his 'mates' (which is what boys in England call their friends).

That was the final straw for Ken Bear's heart. It was as if a ton of bricks had fallen on him, crushing his hope completely. It was his very worst fear, and Gregory's mother had actually said the words out loud! Ken Bear fainted dead away, and the world around him went all black as he sunk into the deepest despair yet. He was a very sad bear, indeed!

3

Ken Bear didn't know how long he had been in darkness, but when he woke up he found himself way up high on a shelf in Gregory's room. There he sat, day after day, watching Gregory play with his mates, his younger brother, James, and with all the other toys and games that filled his room. The worst part of each day was bedtime, when Gregory crawled into bed with another stuffed toy. Ken Bear watched Gregory snuggle it close and give it the love that Ken Bear thought was his alone. Surely watching Gregory give love to other toys was much worse than the fear of going to the rubbish heap would ever be.

One morning, Ken Bear felt his eyes grow dimmer than they had ever been before. It was as if he was looking through a thick fog. As his vision clouded, Ken Bear felt his life-force start to fade away. Without the life-giving touch of a child, all stuffed toys—and especially stuffed bears—will cease to exist. Little did Ken Bear know it, but his eyes weren't cloudy because he was fading away, but because the magic dust, which had come in through the window, had finally worked its way thoughout his insides and he was enshrouded with it. It swirled around him and the world went dim, then disappeared completely, as the magic pulled him into an enchanted mist. What Ken Bear thought was misery and lonliness was actually preparing him for a grand adventure.

Suddenly through the mist, he heard Gregory shouting to him.

What? he thought, giving himself a shake. *Is he talking to me?*

Gregory WAS talking to Ken Bear with great excitement. He bounced around his bedroom shouting that they were all going to see Gramma! Ken Bear became fully alert as Gregory told him that Mother agreed that Ken Bear could, no he must, come along, too. Ken Bear was taken down from his perch, as Gregory's mother cautioned Gregory to be very careful in handling Ken Bear. She called him "threadbare" and "fragile."

Gregory could barely contain his excitement as he told Ken Bear about his Gramma, who lived in a faraway place called "Texas." Gregory was sure that Gramma knew some magic to help Ken Bear get all better before it was too late to save him. Gregory assured Ken Bear that if there was anyone in the entire world that could make Ken Bear whole and happy again, it was Gramma.

As almost anyone can tell you, all grandmothers worth their salt hold within them a generous portion of Grandmother Magic. This magic allows grandmothers to help their grandchildren when the parents have given up, or have told their kids that there is nothing more that can be done. Grandchildren know by instinct that it isn't over until the grandparents have said so, and Gregory happily told Ken Bear that all would be made better by his gramma. All Ken Bear had to do was believe, and then wait and see!

I must tell you, Ken Bear was a bit skeptical about this Grandmother Magic. He had been so sad for so long that his fears had almost completely consumed him. At one time, he would have been thrilled to go to a faraway place called Texas, but now, part of him feared that he would be taken to this strange land and then left behind. The magic dust had prepared him, however, and the hope for Gramma to help was just a teeny bit stronger than his fear, so Ken Bear agreed to go along for the ride.

4

The ride turned out to be long and uncomfortable. On the day they left for Gramma's house, Ken Bear found himself pushed into a small bag. He overheard Gregory's mother call it a "carry-on" bag. It was stuffed with all sorts of odds and ends that Gregory felt he couldn't go to Texas without. After a long drive, they arrived at the international airport in London. Ken Bear strained his ears, listening as they checked in and passed through what was called the "security check." The bag was opened briefly and large, rough hands pushed him to and fro as the man belonging to the hands looked through Gregory's bag.

After the security check, Ken Bear was grateful as Gregory removed him from the bag, so Ken Bear could experience the sights and sounds of a big international airport for the very first time.

Ken Bear was both excited and afraid. There were

so many people, going in so many different directions. The noise was overwhelming, much louder than anything he'd heard before (even louder than when Gregory and his mates got rowdy). It was the scariest place he'd been since the time Gregory had taken Ken Bear to show-and-tell at school.

Just as Ken Bear was getting used to the hubbub of the airport, Gregory pushed him back into the bag so they could board the jumbo jet. Up, up, and away the large airplane climbed into the sky, and off they went to Gramma's house in Texas.

Gregory kept telling Ken Bear that Gramma lived in Texas, but he never bothered to explain that Texas was halfway around the world from where they lived in England! It would take many hours to get there. Another thing Ken Bear didn't understand was what Gregory meant when he said they would be flying. Even he knew that people and stuffed bears couldn't fly.

After what seemed like hours, Gregory finally took Ken Bear out of his carry-on bag. He pressed his shabby face against the airplane window to let Ken Bear look outside. When Ken Bear saw how high up in the sky they were, he nearly lost what little stuffing he had left! He suddenly wished Gregory would just put him back into the carry-on bag. Maybe stuffed bears and people couldn't fly, but apparently airplanes were very good at it. All the same, Ken Bear was sure that he'd rather be inside the bag, just in case. Ken Bear decided then and there that stuffed bears do not enjoy flying. (As it turned out, stuffed bears are not the only ones with a fear of flying, but that is for another story, perhaps best told by Gregory's mother!)

There were lots of people on the airplane. Between watching movies, eating food, and drinking fizzy drinks, Ken Bear had plenty of distractions and soon he almost forgot that they were soaring high above the ocean. Almost. He never really forgot two things; one was that sharks lived in the ocean and were fierce predators, and two was that stuffed bears cannot swim!

He learned all about sharks from listening to Gregory read an article about them from a magazine (a subscription his granddad gave him one Christmas). He learned of his lack of swimming skills firsthand, after numerous encounters with bathtubs, paddling pools, and laundry tubs over the years. Either way, he had no desire to meet predators or to sink to the bottom of the ocean where they lived. So, he tried very hard not to think about it.

Ken Bear got a big new stain on his arm when James spilled some juice on him. With all of the other things already on his sleeve, Ken Bear didn't think anyone would even notice it. During the juice-spilling commotion, Ken Bear noticed that there was a woman across the aisle who was looking at him. She had a strange smile on her face that made Ken Bear feel uneasy. He began to wonder if she was sick, or if her face was stuck like that, when she got up from her seat and reached toward him with her long fingers! If Ken Bear could have yelled out, he would have. He imagined her throwing him out of the plane to the ocean below, where sharks were waiting to gobble him up.

He was relieved, however, when she just touched him gently and began to speak to Gregory's mother. He listened intently (just in case he had to defend himself). He heard her say that she was a grandmother and that her grandson had a stuffed toy that he could not go anywhere without.

The nosy lady went on to advise Gregory's mother that the best thing to be done was to conveniently leave Ken Bear behind in Texas. She told Gregory's mother that eventually Gregory would forget all about him and go on to more age-appropriate toys.

He didn't get to hear Gregory's mother's response to this horrible advice because the stewardess came along and made everyone take their seats and buckle up. Ken Bear was returned to the carry-on bag once again, where he stayed until they arrived at Gramma's house in Texas.

5

Boy, it was hot in Texas! Ken Bear was awfully glad when he was finally taken out of that cramped and stuffy old bag! Now, where was this Gramma that he'd heard so much about?

When Gramma took Ken Bear into her cool hands, Ken Bear experienced something he never experienced before. His mind began to play an old memory, long forgotten and now brought back like he was watching a movie.

He was sitting on a shelf in a small toy shop. The store owner straightened him up and positioned him just so. Throughout the day, many hands picked him up, faces looked him over, and he was repositioned on his shelf. Once, someone returned him to the wrong spot, and that evening the toy owner found him and put him back in his place.

Then, he was put in a special display box. He

heard the shop owner mention something called "Christmas" and he heard him say that all children need a bear to love. Once again he was picked up, pinched, looked over, poked, and rejected as being "too small."

Ken Bear wasn't sure why, but each time he was put back down, his heart felt more and more sad. But then, a wonderful lady appeared. She picked him up and looked into his eyes with her two lovely blue ones. As her cool hands held onto him, he felt safe. She declared that he was, "Just perfect!" and his tiny heart swelled with happiness like he'd never known. A few more times she said it, "He's perfect!"

And he went to live with Gregory.

It was those same blue eyes that looked at him now. This was Gramma!? He couldn't believe it. Ken Bear watched her closely to see if she still thought he was perfect. She smiled at him, and his hope grew a wee bit.

As she put Ken Bear on a shelf in her library, Gramma told Gregory that she'd see what she could do, but wouldn't make any promises.

And there he remained, as everyone came and went, doing all the things that people typically do while on vacation to Gramma's house in Texas. From where he sat, he could look out of the window, into the yard where

Gramma's swimming pool was a source of great fun. He enjoyed watching, but was very glad that stuffed bears were not expected to swim in Texas. As you may recall, Ken Bear already knew for a fact that stuffed bears cannot swim.

Every day seemed more hectic and frantic than the one before. Every now and then, especially when everyone was out, Mr. Dickens and Miss Priss (Gramma's Maine Coon cats) would notice him up on the bookshelf and come over to talk to him. They assured him not to worry because all would turn out well. They said that Gramma had a lot of Grandmother Magic, which they had seen firsthand on numerous occasions.

Ken Bear did worry, though, because the vacation was almost over and Gramma had not even taken a second to look at him since placing him high on the shelf.

Then, just as he feared, Gregory left with his mother, father, and James. They flew back to Number 9 Oaken Grove Lane in England, and Ken Bear was left behind in a strange, hot place called Texas, where people talked funny, big cats roamed about freely, and a very sad, disappointed stuffed bear sat forgotten on a lonely shelf in Gramma's library.

6

At first, Ken Bear remained angry at the nosy lady on the airplane for suggesting such a thing as leaving him behind in Texas. He was sure that it was all her fault. His anger faded into hopelessness and he lost count of the hours as they turned into days. As he sat there untouched, he came to the conclusion that there was no magic for him. Nothing could restore him to his former self, and he had fallen for a nasty trick.

Now, he was far, far from the only home he had ever known and Gregory hadn't even looked sad when he left him behind. He was probably, right that minute, snuggling up to a new stuffed bear with nice, soft fur and no holes and a nose that didn't threaten to fall off. He tried to force himself to be happy for Gregory and told himself that it was the best thing all around, but still his little bear heart ached.

I will give up and live here forever in relative

peace, he decided. After all, it was just too hot and scary to think of doing anything drastic (like jumping off the shelf and trying to make his way back to England). Mr. Dickens and Miss Priss seemed nice enough, but they were cats, after all, and being friends with them wasn't the same thing at all as being loved by Gregory. Besides, he watched how they liked to toss their toys around and pounce on top of them, digging their sharp claws in to hold the toy still. They chewed on their toys with their razor-like teeth. He hoped he wouldn't become one of their toys.

Just as he had this all worked out in his little stuffed-bear brain, Gramma came in and took him down from his perch. She gave him a good looking over and, as she peered and probed, she talked to him.

She told him that she was sad to see him in such a state of disrepair. She said it would be a challenge, but she was working on a plan for some restorative magic for him. She told him to be patient and to search in his heart to start to believe again, or else the magic wouldn't work.

Gramma gently probed his various open areas to see what needed to be done. She told him she was pleased to see that he had a considerable amount of magic dust residing inside of him already, which would certainly be a great help to her. Yes, she said, she was quite pleased and promised to get started on her plan right away.

Gramma came every day after that and talked to him. He listened, but just couldn't fully make himself believe that all would be well. He did, however, begin to let his glimmer of hope grow as the magic dust got stirred up. When magic dust begins to swirl, it can brighten the outlook of even the most skeptical bear.

Ken Bear's little seed of hope was just what Gramma needed to get her own Grandmother Magic to work. She saw that Ken Bear had hope in his eyes once more, and she knew that his hope held enough power for a small miracle, which is what was needed. Time would tell, and she knew she needed to get started with her plan right away.

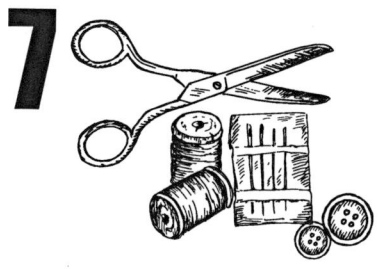

First, she slowly and carefully took all the patches off his torn, bedraggled body. Then she meticulously picked out all the stitching. She laid each piece out on the table and made a pattern by placing the different pieces of his body onto tracing paper and drawing the outline of them. She labeled each piece carefully as she went so she could remember where each piece was meant to be.

Ken Bear was very scared when he realized that all his body parts were scattered about on the tabletop. His head wasn't even connected to his body anymore! His insides were laying in a small heap, waiting for the outside to be replaced. Don't be afraid! Gramma knew how to preserve the magic dust from the old stuffing so that none would be lost in the process.

As Gramma worked on him, she told him what she was doing and why. She told him over and over again that he needed to believe in her magic and all would be well. She said that she would use as many of his original parts as possible, but she would have to get some new material. She told him she was very sorry about this, but he would need to trust her that she would try her best to match the new material with the old. His old material was made of thermal cotton, which was more difficult to find in the hot climate of Texas, especially in the summertime.

That part made him sad. Here he was, in the summertime, in Texas, laying in pieces on Gramma's table. In his gloomy state, he was sure she'd never find the material to restore him.

Through it all, Gramma continued to tell him every day, that it would all be alright. She told him that as he began to see and feel the results, the magic would grow stronger. Very slowly, he started to believe. He reasoned that he had absolutely nothing left to lose by believing. However, if he did not believe, he could lose everything! As his belief grew, he saw the magic grow, too.

One day, Gramma came in with a wonderful announcement. She said that because Ken Bear was such a great believer, she found the needed thermal material. She found it in a shirt that morning at a discount clothing store. The real miracle was that the shirt was brand new and was exactly the right color and from it,

Gramma could make the top half of Ken Bear's body and even the hood for his shirt.

From that moment on Ken Bear knew that all would be well. He now had a heart that not only hoped, but believed and also began to have faith that what he believed would come true.

Mr. Dickens and Miss Priss came by the table where Ken Bear lay in pieces to congratulate him on his soon-to-be new body. They assured him that soon he would be back together again and on his way home to England. Ken Bear was elated to think about going back to England and didn't want to get too excited, since he didn't know exactly when that would happen. It was enough for now to know that Gramma had found the right material and so, as he lay scattered all about on Gramma's table, he repeated over and over again, "I believe, I believe, I believe!"

Hope turned to belief, and belief was turning into faith. Ken Bear was slowly becoming real once again.

8

The day finally came when Gramma told Ken Bear that by nightfall his body would be whole again. He wouldn't have just a "new" body, she said, but a "new and improved" body. She told him she was making everything in double thickness so he wouldn't fray so easily in the future.

As Gramma worked her magic, she sang happy little songs. She told Ken Bear all about how she had been an operating room nurse (or a "theater nurse," as they were called in England) in her younger days. She told him that he could rely on her to put all the pieces together again without causing him too much pain or discomfort. She reminded him that she was also very good at puzzles and so he didn't need to worry his little bear head that any pieces would end up in the wrong places.

Ken Bear found himself laughing along with her

and even learned the words to some of her songs. Before he knew it, a new feeling came over him. It was confidence. He knew, without any doubt whatsoever, that all would be well, just as Gregory and Gramma had both promised. He couldn't wait for the day to be over so he could have his body back once again.

After a while, Gramma said the words he'd been waiting to hear. All of his parts were reconnected! She picked him up and took him over to the mirror so he could have a look at his new and improved self.

What he saw in the mirror amazed him. It was more than he had ever hoped or dreamed for. His whole body looked better than he ever remembered it looking. (Of course, he had been tattered for a long time, and he couldn't really recall what he looked like before.)

He was overjoyed!

But then, he looked more closely at his little bear face. It looked out of place to him on such a magnificent body. He wondered when he had gotten so old. His nose still looked as if it would fall off at any minute. And what about all of the fur that was missing from his cheeks and head? Even with the miracle of a new body, he wondered what, if anything, could be done for his face?

Gramma saw all of this in his eyes and answered him with a beautiful smile. He knew then that she still had some magic left. Before she even spoke the words, he knew she wanted him to keep believing and continue on in faith.

It took almost all of the next day to restore Ken Bear's face. Gramma molded him a new snout by using fabric paint over pantyhose material. She told him that it made him look more mature. It also kept his nose firmly in place, which was a very good bargain. Gramma called it "bear rhinoplasty," and said she wasn't sure any such magic had ever been attempted before. Then she placed some of the pantyhose material under the remaining fabric of his face and stitched it into place. She attached the back of his head and then stitched on the hood.

Gramma filled the gaps on his face where the fur had been rubbed off with fabric paint and then textured it to look like real fur.

It was tedious work and had to be done layer upon layer. Gramma restitched his mouth using the original thread, and it no longer looked lopsided. Finally, Gramma told him that she was finished and there was nothing more she could do. He could tell by her smile that she was pleased.

Ken Bear steeled himself as Gramma picked him up and carried him over to the mirror to see the finished result. He wanted to believe all was well, but in his tiny bear brain he couldn't imagine that the outcome he desired would be the outcome he would see in the mirror.

He closed his eyes really tight. He held his breath and prayed.

Gramma laughed and told him to open his eyes and see for himself before he turned blue and passed out. Ken Bear slowly let out his breath and eased his eyes open. First one. Then the other. He gasped in amazement. Was that really his face? Look how handsome he was! Ken Bear was very pleased indeed!

Gramma saw the joy of life rekindle in Ken Bear's eyes. She knew he was almost complete. He gained more than just a new body and a new face. He had been filled with hope. Then belief. Then faith. And now, joy! Gramma knew there was one thing left to do to make the magic complete. She needed to send him home to Gregory so that love could fill his tiny bear heart once again. Remember, all stuffed bears need the life-giving touch of a loving child in order to exist in this world. To get that loving touch, she needed to send him home.

And that's exactly what I did.

Also by Rosa Frost: *The Best Christmas Wish*

This is a Christmas rhyme that is sure to become a family favorite. It's Christmas Eve and Santa is preparing for his big ride. But wait! A last-minute Christmas wish has just arrived from Alice and Santa can't find her present! Will he make it in time? What will Alice find under her tree?

Touch Publishing
ISBN: 978-1-942508-01-4

Buy it through Amazon, Barnes & Noble, or order through your local book retailer.

CPSIA information can be obtained at www.ICGtesting.com
Printed in the USA
BVOW02s0002190515

400669BV00011B/138/P

9 781942 508106